Toby's Trousers

A humorous story

This edition first published in 2006 by
Sea-to-Sea Publications
1980 Lookout Drive
North Mankato
Minnesota 56003

Text © Anne Cassidy 2004, 2006
Illustration © Jan Lewis 2004

Printed in China

Library of Congress Cataloging-in-Publication Data:

Cassidy, Anne, 1952-
  Toby's trousers / by Anne Cassidy.
    p. cm. — (Reading corner)
  Summary: Harry and Toby, two clowns, go shopping for a new pair of trousers for Toby.
  ISBN 1-59771-009-1
    [1. Pants—Fiction. 2. Clowns—Fiction.] I. Title. II. Series.

PZ7.C26858To 2005
[E]—dc22

                                                    2004064998

9 8 7 6 5 4 3 2

Published by arrangement with the Watts Publishing Group Ltd, London

Series Editor: Jackie Hamley
Series Advisors: Linda Gambrell, Dr. Barrie Wade, Dr. Hilary Minns
Design: Peter Scoulding

Toby's Trousers

Written by
Anne Cassidy

Illustrated by
Jan Lewis

SEA-TO-SEA
Mankato Collingwood London

Anne Cassidy
"I live in London with a very old dog and my son. I like writing about both of them! I hope you enjoy the story!"

Jan Lewis
"I work in a shed in the garden where nobody can see me. So I can wear my favorite old clothes, just like Toby wants to!"

Toby's trousers were old.

"Throw them away,"
said Harry.

"But I like them!" said Toby.

Harry and Toby
went shopping.

"Look at these!" said Harry.

9

"Go and try them on,"
said Harry.

"These are too short!"
said Toby.

"Those are too long!"
said Harry.

15

"These are too tight!"
said Toby.

17

"Those are too baggy!"
said Harry.

19

"These trousers are great!
I like them best," said Toby.

21

"But they are your old trousers!" cried Harry.

23

Notes for parents and teachers

READING CORNER has been structured to provide maximum support for new readers. The stories may be used by adults for sharing with young children. Primarily, however, the stories are designed for newly independent readers, whether they are reading these books in bed at night, or in the reading corner at school or in the library.

Starting to read alone can be a daunting prospect. READING CORNER helps by providing visual support and repeating words and phrases, while making reading enjoyable. These books will develop confidence in the new reader, and encourage a love of reading that will last a lifetime!

If you are reading this book with a child, here are a few tips:

1. Make reading fun! Choose a time to read when you and the child are relaxed and have time to share the story.

2. Encourage children to reread the story, and to retell the story in their own words, using the illustrations to remind them what has happened.

3. Give praise! Remember that small mistakes need not always be corrected.

READING CORNER covers three grades of early reading ability, with three levels at each grade. Each level has a certain number of words per story, indicated by the number of bars on the spine of the book, to allow you to choose the right book for a young reader:

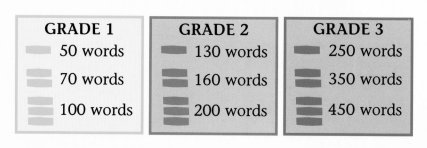

GRADE 1	GRADE 2	GRADE 3
50 words	130 words	250 words
70 words	160 words	350 words
100 words	200 words	450 words